The Crayons in Rainbow Land

by Susan V. Cappelli

and illustrated by Robert Nehrebecki, Jr.

ISBN 978-1-64003-296-5 (Paperback)
ISBN 978-1-64003-297-2 (Digital)

Covenant Books, Inc.
11661 Hwy 707
Murrells Inlet, SC 29576
www.covenantbooks.com

I dedicate this book to my mother who instilled in me the values of love and respect to all people. I also dedicate this book to the children I have taught who inspired me with their joy of learning and with happy memories of teaching.

The Crayons were excited
And thought that it was grand
To spend a special day
In a place called Rainbow Land.

Ruby Red was on her bike,
Racing down the hill.
"Be careful," said Dr. Brown,
"Before you take a spill."

Ruby Red kept racing on,
Like a flying buzzing bee.
She did not even listen
to the doctor's caring plea.

Then something awful happened!
She bumped into a tree.
Dr. Brown came to her aid
And bandaged up her knee.

Now Ruby Red felt better
And with a happy face.
She smiled and thanked the doctor
and promised not to race.

Dazzling Yellow went for a walk.

She met Celinda Blue.

They both sat down and began to talk.

They didn't know what to do.

Then up jumped Celinda Blue,
Excited as could be.
"Let's go to the Crayon Zoo.
It will be a sight to see."

15

As they entered the Crayon Zoo,
An elephant splashed Celinda Blue.
"I'm all wet," she said in a rage.
So she ran to the monkey cage.

Then she laughed. "Oh, it's okay.
I'll dry fast. It's a sunny day."
They saw the lions and tigers too.
It was fun at the Crayon Zoo.

As they were leaving the Crayon Zoo,
A monkey ran to Celinda Blue.
"Oh, please come back with your friend too.
I'll tell my friend not to splash you."

Vernie Green was in the park.

He was playing basketball.

Making shots were quick for him;

He was so lean and tall.

Tangie Orange stood close by.
He wanted to play too.
He ran to Vernie Green and said,
"I'd like to challenge you."

Vernie Green looked down and thought.
"Does he really want to play?
He's no challenge. He's too short.
I'll score high and win today."

Vernie Green did not know
That Tangie Orange was a pro.
Tangie dribbled on the spot
And made a quick three-point shot.

29

Tangie Orange took the lead.
He scored so high today.
Vernie Green shook his hand
In a warm and friendly way.

"Oh, Tangie," said Vernie Green,
"You played so well today.
Join the famous All-Star Team
Of the good old USA."

Benji Black was on roller blades.
He was practicing his spin.
He signed up for a challenge game,
And he would like to win.

When Benji Black had his turn,
He did some tricks and jumped so high.
All the Crayons clapped and cheered.
But the score showed it was a tie.

Benji Black knew what he had to do,
To make his score go high.
He twirled and jumped.
With a nice high fling.
This trick had broken the tie.

Benji Black had won first prize.
Coach Violet said, "It is no surprise.
Benji Black worked hard to win.
He did a difficult flying spin."

Wendy White had a good idea.
She called her friends
To please come near.
"Let's celebrate in a special way
And decorate this tree today."

"Each branch will have a different color:
Red, black, green, white, and yellow too,
Violet, brown, orange, and the color blue.

It's a special tree, so tall and grand.
We'll always remember Rainbow Land."

The Crayons left a message,
On this special tree,
With memories of togetherness,
Respect, and harmony.

They spent a day in Rainbow Land,
With care, fun, and joy.
This wish they now send to
Every girl and boy.

Here are some songs for you to sing with the crayons in The Crayons in Rainbow Land!
Written by Susan V. Cappelli

Ruby Red - Dr. Brown
(Sing to the tune: London Bridge is Falling Down)

Ruby Red now has a friend,
Dr. Brown, a message he sent,
Ruby promised to obey,
Cheers from Ruby.

Obey your parents and teachers too,
They all want the best for you.
Ruby sends this message too,
Cheers from Ruby.

Celinda Blue - Dazzling Yellow

(Sing to the tune: This Old Man)

Celinda Blue, she got wet,
And she was so very upset,
With a click clack, polly pack, dilly dally do,
She got wet at the Crayon Zoo.

Dazzling Yellow, she stood by,
And she whispered, "My oh my",
With a click clack, polly pack, dilly dally do,
An elephant splashed Celinda Blue.

Celinda Blue, thought it through,
It can also work for you,
With a click clack, polly pack, dilly dally do,
All went well for Celinda Blue.

Vernie Green - Tangie Orange
(Sing to the tune: Old MacDonald Had a Farm)

Vernie Green was a very good sport,
Hi Dee, Hi Dee O
When Tangie Orange won the game,
Hi Dee, Hi Dee O
With a dribble, dribble here and
a dribble, dribble there,
Here a throw, there a throw,
Everywhere a throw, throw,
Tangie knew the way to go
Hi Dee, Hi Dee O.

With a dribble, dribble here and
a dribble, dribble there,
Here a throw, there a throw,
Everywhere a throw, throw,
Tangie knew the way to go
Hi Dee, Hi Dee, O

Benji Black - Coach Violet
(Sing to the tune: The Farmer in the Dell)

If you want to reach your goal,
You have to work with zest.
Hi Ho the Merrio,
Just try your very best.

Benji had the will,
To do a special skill.
He didn't say, "I can't, I can't"
He said, "I will, I will."

Coach Violet gave him praise,
He worked so hard to win.
Hi Ho the Merrio,
For Benji's flying spin.

So, try your very best,
No matter where you are.
Hi Ho the Merrio,
And you can be a star.

Wendy White

(Sing to the tune: Mary Had a Little Lamb)

Wendy and her Crayon friends,
Cray O lay, Cray o lay.
Enjoyed the day in Rainbow Land,
O Cray O Day.

They left a message on the Rainbow Tree,
Rainbow Tree, Rainbow Tree.
Blending colors for all to see,
And live in harmony.

Each crayon left a message bright,
To do what's right, to do what's right.
So, let's remember Rainbow Land,
Each message true and grand.

About the Author

Susan Cappelli is a retired teacher from Yonkers, New York. She taught in the Yonkers Public School System. Miss Cappelli holds a bachelor's degree in education from Seton Hall University and a Master's Degree in Education with a specialization in Reading from Potsdam University. She also received the Editor's Choice Award from the National Library of Poetry.

In her spare time, she enjoys reading, traveling, and handcrafts.

CPSIA information can be obtained
at www.ICGtesting.com
Printed in the USA
JSHW040902030721
16531JS00002B/4

9 781640 032965